Elvis Sunny Bear

Boulders, Bridges & Rainbows

* *
* *

by
Michael J. Harris, PhD
&
Catherine M. Edwards

TED E. BEAR PRESS / AUBURN, WA

Ted E. Bear Press
1292 43rd Street NE
Auburn, WA 98002

www.TedEBearPress.com

Publisher's Note: This is a work of fiction. Names, characters, places, and incidents are a product of the author's imagination. Locales and public names are sometimes used for atmospheric purposes. Any resemblance to actual people, living or dead, or to businesses, companies, events, institutions, or locales is completely coincidental.

Special discounts are available on quantity purchases. For details, contact the publisher at the address above.

Auburn, WA / Michael J. Harris, PhD and Catherine M. Edwards

Wake in the deepest dark of night and hear the driving rain.
Reach out a hand and take a paw and go to sleep again.

- Charlotte Gray

CONTENTS

*
* *

1 – OFF TO SEE WALLY!

One sunny day, very late in the spring, Elvis Sunny Bear decided that it was time to go to the seashore to visit his friend, Wally, the whale. He knew that Wally and Wally's family would be there this time of year and he missed him.

It wasn't very far from Elvis's home to where he would meet Wally – the seashore was just on the other side of the mountain from where Elvis lived – but "just on the other side" of anything was quite a ways when you have little bear legs!

Trips to the seashore always needed careful planning. Elvis spent the rest of that day planning and making sure everything he would need would be in his backpack.

Early the next morning he got up, ate his little bear breakfast, said goodbye to his mother and father; his sisters and brothers; and all of his aunts, uncles and cousins. He slung his backpack over his shoulder, waved goodbye and headed off for the seashore.

Like all little brown bears, Elvis found walking to be a very good way to get where he was going. Not only was it great exercise, but it also gave him plenty of time to think and solve the types of problems that little brown bears have. Problems like what to do while all the other bears were sleeping for the winter and he wasn't tired.

As Elvis walked into the forest, he noticed that the path he usually took was very overgrown with weeds, tall grass and even taller sticker bushes. He knew he wouldn't be able to walk very fast – it was like a jungle, and it would take him forever!

This was BIG little bear problem. Elvis needed to get to the seashore soon if he was going to visit with his friend Wally while he was still there. Wally is a humpback whale, and humpback whales are headed north at this time of year to their summer fishing grounds. If he took too long to get to the seashore, Wally wouldn't be there!

*
* *

2 – WHICH WAY?

He set his backpack down and looked around and he saw the start of another path. It looked like this one went up and over the mountain instead of around it. It really wasn't as nice as the path he usually took - it was rocky and uneven, dusty and very steep.

Elvis thought about it for a few moments and decided, since there were no sticker bushes, that he'd try it! He scooped up his backpack, took one last look around and up the new trail he hiked.

The trail went up and up - and up some more. The higher he hiked, the more he noticed that he was getting hotter and dustier.

After a very long while, Elvis realized that the trees were getting smaller and smaller – and smaller.

They went from very tall, to tall, to about the same height as him. Then they were shorter and shorter still – and then there were no more trees!

As he rounded a corner of the trail, he saw that a huge boulder was blocking the way. The left side of the trail dropped off straight down the mountain – he couldn't get past that way! On the other side of the boulder, there was no trail – only a cliff going straight up the mountain! Elvis looked all around, but could see no way to get past the boulder.

He thought of going back down the mountain to the path he normally took – but it was too far and he didn't have time. Elvis wondered what to do?

He sat down at the side of the trail for a think. After a little bit he noticed the shape of the boulder was a little odd. So odd, that when the wind blew... the boulder rocked back and forth a little bit. Little gusts of wind caused it to rock back and forth a little. Bigger gusts of wind caused it to rock back and forth even more.

Elvis went to the boulder and pushed it hard with his paw. It rocked back and forth several times. He pushed it again harder and he noticed that it would move a long way before it slowed and settled back into its resting position.

So Elvis pushed it again – really hard - and he slipped past it and was on his way! Elvis made a mental note to come back someday and move the boulder off the trail… but not today, he had somewhere he needed to be. He continued up the trail and noticed that it was even hotter and dustier on this side of the boulder.

*
* *

3 – DOWNHILL ALL THE WAY?

Finally, he was at the top of the mountain and headed quickly down the other side. It was much easier going down the mountain than it had been going up – and he was making up for all of the time he'd lost earlier. He knew that the quicker he got to the seashore, the more time he could spend visiting with Wally!

As he headed down the mountain, the trees got taller and taller and taller. Soon, there were so many trees he could only see the trail ahead of him. When he rounded a bend in the trail where there were no trees, he could see the seashore off in the distance and he was sure he could see whales swimming just offshore!

Down at the bottom of the mountain he could see a bridge that he would soon have to cross. When he was almost at the bridge, he realized that something just didn't look right – that something was missing. That something was the middle of the bridge! This was definitely a problem.

He knew there was no way to cross the bridge with its middle missing. The river that ran under it looked deep and the water was moving too fast – it was too dangerous for a little bear to try to swim across!

Elvis needed get to the other side of the river to see Wally, but he couldn't. He thought of the mountain trail he had taken. It was a very long way to go back and take his regular path. There was also that big boulder. Could he squeeze past it again? He sat down on a mossy rock for a few minutes for another think.

Just as he was about to turn around and head back the way he had come, he had an idea. All he needed to make the idea work was a rainbow. His Father had once told him that rainbows were magical. He could definitely use a magical rainbow right now!

Elvis looked up, he looked down, and he looked from side to side. He looked all around, but there were no rainbows in sight. Elvis smiled to himself, remembering something his mother had once shown him – how to make a rainbow by holding a bottle of water up to the sun. Would it work? It was worth a try!

Elvis reached into his backpack, took out his bottle of water and held it up to the sun. He had to turn it a bit – a little this way and some that way – before he got it just right. There was bright flash and there, on the ground in front of him, was a rainbow - just where it should be!

Working quickly, Elvis tied one end of the rainbow to the bridge railing next to him where he was standing. Using his best granny knots, the ones grandma bear had taught him, he tied the other end of the rainbow to a rock and tossed it across the hole in the bridge's middle.

It wrapped itself around and around the railing on the other side. Elvis gave it a couple of good strong pulls – just to make sure it was good and tight. Then he picked up his backpack and went quickly across the rainbow bridge to the other side!

4 – ALMOST THERE!

Elvis hadn't gone very much farther up the trail before it met up with the path he usually took and he was able to make it down the trail and to the shore very quickly.

Elvis could see Wally out in the water past the rocks. He jumped up and down and waved his arms to make sure Wally saw him.

Wally saw him and leaped high out of the water. He came down with a very big splash, waved his flipper in the air at Elvis! He did that a couple times to wave Elvis down the beach and onto the rocks.

The rocks went way out into the deep water. Elvis could keep dry and out of the water, and Wally could swim right up to him. It was perfect!

Wally and Elvis both had so much to tell each other that they both started talking at the same time! They realized what happened so they both suddenly stopped talking. When Elvis saw that Wally wasn't talking – he started again, just as Wally did!

As Elvis ate his lunch, Wally told him all about his recent adventures. He and his whale family had been hanging out just offshore for several weeks. The weather was good and the fishing was great! There was lots of time for the whole family to play. They both agreed whales and little bears have the same favorite things – to eat and play all day!

Then, it was Elvis's turn. He filled Wally in on his cousins' new home, how his dad taught him how to swim at the local pond, and all about his new neighbors – the little bear family with nothing but girls.

Wally asked Elvis how his trip to the seashore had been that morning. He told Wally how the path he usually took was blocked, but how he'd found a new trail. He explained how he'd squeezed past the boulder blocking the trail. Then Elvis showed Wally how he made a rainbow and used it to cross the broken bridge.

"That was quite the trip, and you solved all of this morning's problems before they became BIG problems – just by using your inner bear wisdom!" Wally said. "I hope your trip home will be much smoother."

"Well, I am definitely NOT taking the trail up over the mountain on my way home today," Elvis replied. "I'll find some way to get through the weeds, tall grass and sticker bushes when I get there."

Wally chuckled. "You don't need to worry about that!" he said, and pointed past Elvis with his flipper. "Look at that piece of driftwood over by that rock. Does that look a lot like a baseball bat to you?"

Elvis looked at the piece of driftwood. "Yes, it does look like a baseball bat."

"Well", Wally answered, "You can always use a driftwood kind of baseball bat on those weeds and sticker bushes and pretend you're getting ready for a baseball tryout".

5 – TIME TO GO!

Just as Elvis was packing his things back in his backpack, Wally's mother called out that it was time to leave. The rest of Wally's family had arrived and they would be leaving for Alaska very soon.

Wally and Elvis said their goodbyes and Elvis gave Wally a BIG little bear hug, picked up his driftwood bat, slung his backpack over his shoulder, and headed to the pathway home.

At the top of a little hill, Elvis turned and waved goodbye to Wally and his whole family. They all waved back and he knew they'd all be seeing each other soon.

Walking home that afternoon, Elvis thought about how little bear problems are more easily solved before they become big little bear problems.

As Elvis was going home on the path through the forest, swatting sticker bushes and pretending to hit the game winning home run, he decided that tonight while he was sleeping and dreaming he would remember this day.

And, he was going to remember that sometimes

problems only look like problems until you get on the other side of them. And to solve your problems you just need to use your inner bear wisdom to push on the boulders and make rainbows into bridges until you are where you need to be.

And that is the End
of *this* adventure!

ABOUT THIS BOOK

We feel that developmental learning in children and adolescents is timeless, and that the skills needed for that development is best absorbed through stories. With the days of stories being "told around the camp fire" and of tribal or large family learning sets being long since past; the necessity of teaching these learning sets and ancestral stories is more important than ever. However, the necessity of teaching learning sets is more important than ever.

In addition to being entertaining, this title and the other stories in the 'Elvis Sunny Bear' series from Ted E. Bear Press are designed specifically to provide a methodology for parents, teachers and children to address different, and sometimes uncomfortable, topics in a way that is respectful and informational without having to be too scientific or direct – yet still provide needed resources and education.

ABOUT US

Please visit us at http://www.TedEBearPress.com for information about Ted E. Bear Press, view author and contributor biographies, and to see the adventures our little bear family has in store for the children of the world!

Made in the USA
San Bernardino, CA
09 November 2015